Anthony Masters

The Sea Horse

Illustrated by James Mayhew

MACDONALD YOUNG BOOKS

Chapter One

The waves were getting bigger and Jamie was afraid. He should never have tried to swim when the sea was so rough. But when he had come down to the cove on his own so early in the morning the waves had looked safe.

Once he was out amongst the white horses – the crests that were full of foam – he could feel how strong they were. They dashed back on to the beach and then pulled him out again. Each time, the waves pulled him out even further. Soon the safe sand was a long way away.

Jamie began to panic. Kicking and fighting, he tried desperately to struggle back to the beach. He swallowed water and realised how stupid he had been to come into the sea alone; he wasn't even a strong swimmer. The more scared he became, the more he struggled; and the more he struggled, the more water he swallowed.

Jamie knew that he was getting weaker, and
if someone didn't rescue him soon he would
surely drown. He thought of Mum and Dad
and his little sister Gemma, and began to cry.
He looked back to the beach, but there was
no one there to hear his calls. Even so, Jamie
began to shout for help.

It was no good. Each wave that carried
him towards the sand roared over his head,
and then, with a tremendous wrench, pulled
him out to sea again.

It was rather as if the white horses were playing with him, not understanding that he was some poor human being who couldn't stand up to them – and who was soon going to drown.

Jamie began to sink and to swallow more water. Each time he came up, spluttering and feeling sick. He had never been so frightened in his life. Then he went down again, and this time it seemed that he wouldn't come up.

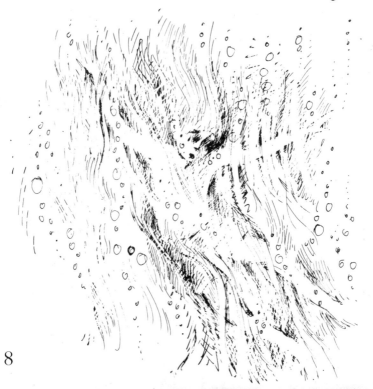

Jamie opened his eyes and saw a light
green world full of bubbles, and there was an
awful sucking sound in his ears.

Suddenly he felt something firm under
him – something very powerful and rather
like the back of the horse that he had ridden
last Easter at the riding stables – but a horse
couldn't be here, not underwater. He was
definitely going up. Jamie could see the
green water streaming away behind him, as
he broke surface with a great splash.

The sun seemed to be very large above
him and it was warm – oh, so beautifully
warm, welcoming him back to the world.
    But when Jamie looked down he was
amazed. He was riding on a white horse.

10

The horse had a foamy mane and a long nose that blew out spray. Although the rest of the Sea Horse's body was still buried in the waves, Jamie could feel its strength. He clung to the mane and was surprised to find that it was just like the thick coarse hair of the horse from the riding stables.

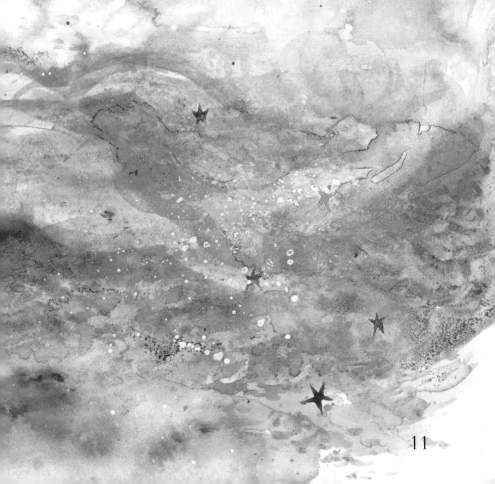

Now the Sea Horse was plunging towards the shore and Jamie had the glorious sensation of almost flying. He saw that around him were dozens of other white horses, all with deep green eyes and foamy manes.

The wind sang in his ears, the sun shone down brightly, and the horses made a wild roaring sound as they hurtled towards the golden sand on the beach.

The Sea Horse reared up in a blaze of
spray and glistening wave, and Jamie could
now see his long legs and strong hooves
pawing the air. Then the Sea Horse lowered
his neck and Jamie slid into the soft water of
the shallows.

Jamie looked up, dazed. The Sea Horse
was galloping back into the sea and
swimming hard to catch up with his friends.
His eyes were a deep green, too – much
darker than the colour of the sea. Jamie
watched him rolling out with the waves as
far as he could see, until he disappeared
towards the horizon.

As Jamie walked back across the beach to his Cornish holiday home, he looked at his watch and saw that it was almost seven. The sun had dried him, so that he could put on his shirt. There were a few people coming down now – a bait-digger, a jogger, a woman with her dog and a boy flying a kite in the stiff breeze.

As he climbed over the sea wall and ran towards the old stone house, Jamie knew that he couldn't tell his parents. He was sure that they wouldn't believe him. He was also sure they would be very angry with him for bathing in a rough sea on his own.

'You haven't been swimming, have you, Jamie?' asked Mum, who was making breakfast.

'No.'

'But you're wet.'

'I was paddling on the edge when a wave splashed me.'

'It's rough today; you can see those white horses dashing in. That's when it's dangerous.

I've told you before. Now promise me that you won't go near the sea again on your own, even when it's calm. I know you like to get up early and explore, but you're not to go down to the cove.'

'No, Mum,' said Jamie, his mouth full of cornflakes. He'd never felt so hungry before. As he ate, he thought about the Sea Horse that had rescued him. *His* Sea Horse.
For the rest of the day Jamie hugged his secret to himself. If only he could make friends with his rescuer and go riding over the waves with him – that would be fantastic.

At lunch time Jamie's family had a picnic on the beach. The wind was fierce and the waves were bigger.

'There's a big storm forecast,' said Dad. 'I'm going to light a fire tonight – keep us nice and warm. Do you want to help Gemma and me look for driftwood, Jamie?'

'You bet,' he replied. It would be fun to have a fire in the old fireplace. He would stare into it and see more horses leaping in the flames.

Chapter Two

The storm started in the afternoon. The sun disappeared, the sky went purple and the wind blew itself into a gale. Rain came and went, and when it had finally gone the whole family stood on the wet sand, watching the raging sea and the dancing, foaming white crests that Jamie knew as his friends – the white horses.

Later, when Jamie went to bed, glowing from toasting marshmallows round the driftwood fire, he opened his window to say goodnight to his Sea Horse.

The sea had surged right up the beach, and the gale was making it pound at the sea wall that was a few metres in front of the house. The waves were gigantic, towering up with their manes and deep green eyes. Then he saw an enormous white horse on the horizon, roaring towards the wall, almost flying as it rose and rose from the other crests until it did fly. Jamie could actually see the horse's legs and hooves as its elegant glistening body soared over the stone house.

Next morning, the beach was storm-lashed with much more driftwood, hanks of rope, part of a fisherman's net, two plastic buckets and an awful lot of stranded starfish. The sea was dead calm and there were no white horses at all.

'Horse broke loose,' said Dad at breakfast. He had just come in from his morning run.

'What sort of horse?' asked Gemma through a mouthful of Marmite toast.

'A big white horse. Must have broken out of its stable during the storm.'

'Where is it now?' asked Mum.

'Sam Gibbons caught it; he's keeping it in his barn.'

'Isn't he that man with the caravans? The one who shouted at Jamie when he went to look at those puppies?' said Mum.

'He didn't seem nice,' agreed Dad, as Mum starting on the washing-up.

'I managed to get a close look at the horse,' he continued. 'It's a wonderful creature. He must have run along the beach at some point.'

Something surged in Jamie's mind. 'Run along the beach?'

'I could smell the salt.'

'What colour were the white horse's eyes, Dad?' asked Jamie urgently.

'Deep green,' his father replied. 'Funny – I've never seen a horse's eyes that colour before.'

Jamie went off on his own after breakfast, pretending he was going to try out his new roller blades on the forecourt of an abandoned filling station. It was conveniently near Sam Gibbons's run-down farm. All Sam's fields were full of caravans now, but he tried to make a bit of extra money with some pigs which he kept in the old farmyard.

No one was around when Jamie arrived at
the farm, but when he crept into the yard he
could see no sign of his Sea Horse.

Then he heard a very light whinny —
almost like the sighing of the wind — coming
from one of the old barns that were so
tumbledown they looked as if they would
collapse at any moment. It was amazing that
they had somehow survived last night's
storm.

28

The whinny came again, and, checking
that there was still no one around, Jamie
darted across the muddy farmyard to the
barn. Inside was the white horse, tethered in
a stall.

He looked very miserable, but it was his
Sea Horse all right, with his deep green eyes
and foamy mane.

'Don't worry,' Jamie whispered to him.
'I'll save you – like you saved me.'

Jamie squeezed into the stall and leant his head against the Sea Horse's flank, breathing in the wonderful smell of seaweed and brine.

Then he tried to untie the halter, but the knot was too tight. He began to panic. It should be so simple. All he had to do was to get the Sea Horse out of the barn, and lead him down the lane to the beach. Then he could plunge into the sea again.

He was searching for some kind of sharp edge to cut the rope on when he heard a loud voice.

'Oi! What do you think you're doing?'

Sam Gibbons stood at the entrance to the barn, looking angry.

'Well?'

'I just came to see the horse.'

'Yours, is it?'

'Not exactly,' said Jamie, not knowing how to explain.

'What do you mean by that? Do your parents own him?'

'No.'

'Do you know who does? I'm looking after him until the owner comes to claim him. He must have escaped in the storm.'

How could Jamie explain that no one
owned the Sea Horse, that he was part of a
wave, wild and free? Sam Gibbons would
only laugh.

'No,' he replied lamely.

'So you just came out of curiosity, did
you?' Gibbons's voice was suspicious.

'I came to see him,' said Jamie stubbornly.
'You ought to let him go,' he added bravely.

'And have him killed on the road?'

'He'd find his own way home.'

'Are you an idiot? Some city-bred idiot?'
Gibbons was even angrier now. 'Haven't you
kids got any understanding of how to look
after animals? You're trespassing on my
property. Clear off!'

Jamie said nothing. There was nothing
more he could say.

'Get out!' Gibbons stood aside to let him
pass. 'And if I see you here again I'll call the
police.'

Jamie ran through the barn door as fast as he could, without a backward glance at the Sea Horse, who gave a sad whinny.

'I'll save you,' Jamie yelled when he had put a safe distance between himself and Sam Gibbons. 'I'll save you.'

Chapter Three

Jamie ran down to the beach, but the sea was still calm. There were no white horses, and the chances of rescuing the Sea Horse seemed hopeless.

He saw his father fishing, and went up to him. 'Is it going to get rough again later?'

'You bet it is,' said his father. 'There's another storm coming tonight. We'll have to move upstairs.'

'Upstairs?'

'There's going to be a very high tide. The coastguards have given out a warning. Don't worry, we'll be OK. I'll sandbag all the doors and board up the lower windows.'

'Who controls the tides, Dad?' asked Jamie.

'The moon,' he replied.

That night, as Jamie looked out of his
bedroom window, he saw that the white
horses had returned. Above him were rolling
thunder clouds and the waxy face of the full
moon. Without thinking, Jamie opened his
window and called out, '*Please* save my Sea
Horse. Please save him.'

Nothing happened, and when he had
called and called for ten minutes Jamie felt a
complete failure. How foolish he had been
to shout at the moon! How his friends would
have laughed at him if they had known! If
only he could have untied the Sea Horse and
led him back to the sea.

It was almost midnight when Jamie,
pausing only to collect his penknife to cut
the tether, gently lowered himself on to the
shed roof from his bedroom window. From
there he could easily slip to the ground.

The wind was howling, the rain was spitting and the white horses were roaring at the sea wall. Was it high tide yet? Somehow he didn't think it was.

Feeling scared, Jamie arrived at the farm, only to see that the Sea Horse had somehow broken free of his tether and was standing stamping his feet at the door of the barn.

Sam Gibbons was there too, trying to force him back inside by cracking a huge whip.

'Stop that!' yelled Jamie.

But Gibbons didn't hear him, and went on lashing at the Sea Horse with his whip.

Then Jamie heard a great roaring sound behind him. When he turned round he saw an enormous wave pouring over the sea wall and hurtling towards him.

When Sam Gibbons saw the huge wave he ran to higher ground, yelling out to Jamie to join him. But Jamie stayed where he was.

As the water swept in, the Sea Horse leapt for joy. With a wild cry he jumped into the wave, which began to curl back to the sea.

The wave had poured over Jamie too, sucking him down, but suddenly he felt the Sea Horse under him, taking him up to the surface. As his head rose above the water he saw that other waves had poured over the wall, and there was masses of white foam on the enormous crests. Safe on the Sea Horse's back, Jamie galloped towards the beach, surrounded by dozens of white horses.

The Sea Horse gently laid Jamie on the sea wall. Then he plunged away towards the horizon.

Quietly, Jamie managed to climb on to the shed, and back through the bedroom window. As he rubbed himself down, he listened to his mother and father talking in the next room.

'Tide's on the turn now, thank goodness,' Dad was saying.

'Glad the kids are safe,' Mum replied.

As Jamie sat on the edge of his bed, he realised he was still holding something. It was a piece of pure white horse hair.

Look out for more enthralling titles in the Storybooks series:

The Saracen Maid by Leon Garfield

Young Gilbert Beckett is captured by pirates and sold to a rich Eastern merchant. While in captivity, he falls in love with the merchant's beautiful daughter . . .

Thomas and the Tinners by Jill Paton Walsh

Thomas works in the tin mine where he meets some fairy miners who cause him a great deal of trouble – but then bring good fortune.

Princess by Mistake by Penelope Lively

What would you do if, one ordinary afternoon, your sister were suddenly kidnapped by a knight and carried away to a castle?

The Midnight Moropus by Joan Aiken

At midnight, on the eve of his birthday, Jon waits at the waterfall to see if the ghost of a long-dead moropus will appear.

The King in the Forest by Michael Morpurgo

While a boy, Tod rescues a young fawn from the King's huntsmen. Many years later, Tod finds his loyalty to his old friend the deer put to the test . . .

All these books and many more in the Storybooks series can be purchased from your local bookseller. For more information about Storybooks, write to: *The Sales Department, Macdonald Young Books, Campus 400, Maylands Avenue, Hemel Hempstead HP2 7EZ.*